DRAMATIS

PERSONAE

DRAMATIS PERSONAE

JEANNELLE M. FERREIRA

PRIME BOOKS

DRAMATIS PERSONAE

Prime Books

www.prime-books.com

for Sonya

DRAMATIS PERSONAE

Snow was rising.

Helices of petal-white spiraled up into the dark of morning, but Julian was conscious only of running in snow ankle-deep, over street grates and street men gilded in ice and when Julian tripped, finally, and went flying, it was over something soft that gave a curse.

Left behind after a scuffle was a water-spotted tawny leather coat, a spool of thread bleeding black into the snow, and a card, one edge thumbed over.

JULIAN SIBLE, it read, **MASKS.**

"You've done it again, haven't you?"

"Done?"

"It's snowing up!" Julian threw down her bag, spilling damp silks and frost-tarnished foils across a pile already leaning. "You can't keep on like this, Isley. They'll come for you, you know they will."

Isley shifted only minutely, enough to reach up and

draw ice crystals from Julian's hair. "There will always be a *they*."

"Is that supposed to be comfort?"

"Darling, Lady Jane Sybilla Grey is the lessee of this apartment, and they haven't caught on to us yet. I'm going to sign you as Medea Malefica Moon-Unit next—" With a long fond sigh Isley shifted again, light and shadow rearranging against the windowpane. "If I don't make something interesting happen—Julian, confection, pearl past price, now listen, floppet—then there isn't any inspiration, and serving the Goddess alone doesn't pay bills." Two pale hands, plump and lined but still with fine-balanced, delicate fingers, reached to cradle Julian's chin. Today they were studded with a Victorian widow's onyx and malachite rings.

"You called me floppet," Julian drew back. "Die."

Somewhere out of reach now, Isley tut-tutted. Really in character, Julian thought, a dowager empress today. Benevolence help us.

"You would age centuries less if only you stayed calmer," Isley was crooning. "Look, I thought up a simply marvelous design while you were out, just look. Just for a minute."

"No." Julian brushed her skinned palms over the seat of her jeans, wincing. "I'm going upstairs. None of your designs are finding their way onto my desk while I'm up there, understand?"

"But this one's a whole panoply, dear—"

"Later. I promise you I will look later." The lager some student had pressed on her at the pub was rising against her ribs. Isley was silent, somewhere invisible in her line of sight; Julian's mind sketched in the capable, marshmallowy male shape Isley usually wore. "And for pity's sake don't leave here without a face."

The field of her vision was clementine-colored. Julian opened one eye a lash wider and found Isley's fingernail, lacquered sunny orange, pressing the tip of her nose. She had fallen asleep in one of her masks, then; and there was sunlight in the sewing room, and the twist of her spine and hips on the old horsehair couch was painful.

"You're late opening up the shop."

When she heard it, the last sleep fled. Julian sat up, slowly, leaving her breath somewhere in the springs of the couch.

Today Isley had shape and gender. A small, neat-handed woman with blue eyes—some of those lapis chips we found in the plaza in Peru—and hair the color of milk in tea. Most of it was drawn up under a kerchief, and the kerchief was safety cone orange, but Julian saw it linen, saw it white.

She made herself know it was Isley, and cocked back a fist, and punched Isley in the face.

Papier-maché gave a damp crunch as the mask and its makings were broken.

"You are entirely too excitable," Isley seemed to speak from the pile of rust and russet clothing that lay on the floor like

9

dead snake skin. The broken mask hovered four feet off the floor, resting on the tips of fingers Julian couldn't see. It was an old mask, two, three centuries now past its crafting, and fine grayish dust eased into the air and danced on light. The room was stuffy, swathed as it was in bolts and folds of fabric. It was far too hot. The mask's lapis eyes were whitened with heat. At Julian's hairline began a teardrop's worth of sweat.

She couldn't force her voice from between her teeth. She had nothing to say to nothing, a shimmering heat and a pile of clothes.

"Julian, love—" There was a nervous flutter in the room, birds alighting on flame, and then Isley popped into view, wearing a half-sewn Green Man, with leafy curls and bright eyes the color of hazelnut shells. "There. Better?"

Julian gripped the broken mask, too cautious to pull. "That's mine. Give it to me."

"You know how I am, Julian. I didn't even look to see what I put on. I just—you know—brain of a tree sloth—I don't think you had better do that!" He finished in a rush.

Julian had already shed last night's mask. She raised the broken one, set it in place and looked out through her new eyes.

She smoothed her hands along her cheekbones. Blood surprised her, and pain. "Broken," she murmured, just to hear the voice, as she felt over her nose. "I didn't mean that. I'm sorry."

Julia?

Julian heard the voice this time without speaking a word; it came on a strand of smoke that moved past her cheek, and she got the stinging smell of burning wool into her nostrils, but she kept no wool in the sewing room, it brought moths, and moths hurt the masks, and it was hot, it was terribly hot.

Julia! Julia!

"Julian!" Isley was shouting at her, wrenching at her hair and her ears, and when Julian shed the mask she lay for a long time, staring at the ceiling, listening only to her own breathing.

"Where the hell did you go?" Isley found her hand, somehow, and squeezed it.

"I burned the mask. I—I must have. It remembered burning."

For once there was none of the buttery British aristocrat in Isley's voice. Without affectation it was a plain, service-able, sweet sort of tenor, though Julian hated the words. "We're not allowed to burn our designs, You know that as well as I." And somehow then he found her forehead, without a mask to guide him, and kissed there.

Julian shoved him, and the Green Man slipped to one side. "I burned it! I burned it!"

"Love," Isley said. "You've got it wrong. They burned—"

But she would not stay to hear anything else.

She sat cross-legged in a sea of flaked jade, choosing scales that would dangle from thread-of-silver netting for the throat and shoulders of a mermaid. This early in the day, only commuters descending from the elevated trains passed by the shop; there was a waft in the room of vinegar, onions, old soup and new bread. Julian did not need to eat, strictly speaking, but the yeasty smell from the Polish restaurant was enough to make her recall hunger. She shared a wall with the restaurant's kitchen; when she leaned against it, now, it was warm.

"You know what I love about this century?" Isley thrust the glass door open so that the bell overhead jangled fiercely. "The fact that one can acquire borscht, injera and green banana salad all in fifteen minutes'—perambule."

"I don't think that's a word," Julian said mildly, never looking up from the borer and the newest piece of jade. It had chipped into a curve perfect as a fingernail, and the light seemed to catch some iridescence on its upper arc. Its flash reminded her of fishes' scales, darting and peeking, swerving safe beneath the uppermost skin of the sea.

"Has to be." Isley swallowed a plastic forkful of plantain, setting down two foam bowls sealed with rubber bands and wax paper. "One perambulates, so naturally the noun form thereof is a perambule."

Julian blew the last traces of jade dust from her work before knotting it onto a strand of silver thread. "Is that where you were, then? For two hours? Or aren't you going to tell me?"

"A man has to have some secrets, my divinity, even in this informational age."

"Infor—" she started to correct him, and quit. "The History of Rasselas, Prince of Abyssinia?"

"Oh, you know how it is. You buy the latest release and somehow never get around to reading it . . . The lady doth ply her needle too much, I think." Isley set the book down and spent two full minutes rubbing his hands on a scrap of batik cotton, scrubbing down into the creases where fingers met palm. Then he drew the pile of work off Julian's lap. "You work too hard, poppet. You've been on this mad ethical streak ever since we moved here."

"It's nothing to do with ethics. I just—I want to be sure all the masks are finished, before we leave."

"You never worried about that before."

"Maybe that's why something always goes wrong." Julian glared. "I want to leave in the Goddess' good time, for once, instead of our usual moonlight flit!"

He had no retort for that; he stretched and folded and re-folded his newly clean fingers, and stared very hard into the cuticles. After a long while he asked his knuckles, "Are you all right? Julia?"

"I'm tired of being driven out." She stood up and found her full height, or at least her height as she remembered it, in the far-buried part of her brain that was not mask-maker. She came to Isley's chin, quite a tall woman for her time.

"We've been doing this for nine hundred years, Isley, and never three months in the same place. Is it getting through to you yet that maybe something is not right?" She managed it, then. Maskless she stood in front of Isley, and for the first time in centuries his eyes followed her. She knew the image was powdery, faint, by now; wavering like a torn-up cloak in the wind, and it was possible that from the waist down she had forgotten herself entirely. But from his expression she knew there were hands, a face, eyes and lips for him to follow, and she remembered the feel of bad linsey-woolsey twill well enough to clothe herself in it.

He didn't recognize her. "Julian—confection—"

"Julia Sybilla Wyckes," she corrected, "very tired. Wanting to change this. All right?"

"Right." Isley's voice seemed to flake away like frail stone.

"We've got to do things as we were told to do in the beginning. A mask for any who needs one, and each mask finished."

"For heaven's sake, poppet, who are we to say a thing is finished?" He mimicked her inflection, though he stumbled a little on the broadness of her accent. "While we're talking of rules, here's another: no mask is finished until it finds the wearer."

"Then we're just going to stay here until all of them get found." Her head was starting to ache. Sound rose and fell so that she could nearly see the waves. "All of them. No matter how long it takes. I'm going to stick in one place and know for once that I haven't damn well fucked every bleeding thing up."

"What, and get shot to bits by the cluck-clucks clan, or the neighborly neo-Nazis, or some other friendly organization? I do hope you remember how it ended last year in Prague!"

"I remember everything," she said, and it wasn't a lie, nearly. "How else do you think I make the masks?"

"I never knew how you did it, truth be told. Myself, I don't think anything at all, if I can help it. I find remembering things to be nearly as messy a business." Coolly he peeled back the lid of one cup of borscht. The borscht had cooled too. With one long, fine fingernail he broke the surface tension and stirred, not looking at Julian. "If it's all pain, poppet, for heaven's sake go and chuck yourself off a bridge. One quick splash or an express bus and it's all done with."

"You don't think I've tried?" Her voice frayed and the dim image broke and the hedge-girl was gone, just a glimmer of motion in Isley's sight.

"Bloody hell!" Isley put down his soup and grabbed up a mask from her work pile, not cleaning his hands this time. Magenta droplets like strange-hued blood seeped through layers of chiffon. "Oh, bloody hell!" But he thrust it at her all the same, and seconds later he faced a dryad in rippling green. "I suppose for the next nine hundred years, we're to do things your way instead of my way. Right! Fine! On your head be it, when I get killed! It's not like I'm the master and you're the apprentice, or anything, oh, no. I suppose one must get to work straight away, with no lunch." He fumbled in the pocket of his purple sateen overalls and came up with a white lawn handkerchief, sprigged, starched, monogrammed with I. "Only leave off crying, darling, please."

"Who was the last person you loved?"

Isley sucked on a cherry stone for a moment before flicking it into the paper bag of fruit. "Um," he said, and the stem followed, done into a perfect knot. "Love, my dulcet, is like a perpetual plague year. It's an emotional state to which I am no longer maintaining my subscription."

Julian's hands went still, twined at the heart of a chunk of clay. "I didn't ask that."

He dipped his handkerchief into the fizzing glass at his side, then drew it over his fingertips, blotting off cherry juice. His hands dried, he rose and he picked up a yard of nearly transparent white kidskin, and he was still silent.

"Isley." Julian set aside the vague facial ovoid that had formed, easily as she breathed, from the dull-colored clay.

"Bring   me   a   number   ten   needle,   the three-oh-three-three silk, two moss agates for inlay and—mohair," he paused, eyes closed, his mouth like a knife. "Mohair in caramel, not honey."

She waited without speaking, scrubbing bits of clay into crumbs that pattered onto the floor.

"And   one   of   your   clay—no.   It   will   have   to   be papier-maché. It must be light," Isley murmured, pacing. His silk smoking jacket opened around him, billowing loose as frail wings. "You'll have to hold still," he said at last. "I need your face."

She could feel her own brows draw down, then up again in surprise. "Can't you—I mean, why don't you do some sculpting on a maché cast that's ready? I have some in the cloth room. Then you could get right to the work—"

"The work?" He bunched up the fine leather in his hand, so that she winced. "What? It's your bones I need; those fine little bird's bones you used to have— Don't stand there and talk to me about the work. You think the sewing and the stitching and the prettiness is the work, don't you? You want me to get right down to it?" His voice was low and fevered. "But it's the bones are the thing, my lovely, the lines in the bones in the face."

She held still for the casting, the gentle wet slap of thick paper across her face—the hedge-girl face she remembered, to her own mind rather like a fox just run up hard against the chicken-house door, all freckles and skimmed-milk skin framed about by a nothing shade of brown. The face was faint. It was hard to keep it from wavering, flickering out altogether beneath Isley's hands.

She sat still while he waited, fists clenched around a sweat-darkened rag, and he made the air around the mask-mold humid with the scent of champagne and cherries. It was a long time to be silent and still; in her head she recited lists of plant-names and stone-names and the names of the sea and sky.

The paper-and-paste cast was still damp when Isley took it by the edges into his hands. The white kidskin smoothed its wrinkles out over cheeks, nose and chin; he thrust a few basting stitches down into the papier-maché, so that Julian saw a dead face with the sheet drawn up, white held steady by white. She had not seen Isley's little pearl-handled work knife in over a year, but it was deadly sharp in his hand now, and it flashed through the delicate leather with more speed than she would ever have dared. The face had its breath now, spaces for sight and speech.

The Isley she knew worked slowly, fastidious and fussing, tut-tutting absurd little songs to the mask cradled across his lap. He was a soft-edged, gliding presence, and he never rushed the work. As she watched him now he looked fierce and compact as a cat; he had sliced his fingers wide with the needle, the silk whistled as he drew stitches faster than breath, and his own mask was slipping, so that his form was silver-edged as he hunched over his work.

When it fell from him completely, Julian shouted, maybe his name, maybe just a sound with no edges to make a word. She could hear him breathing. There was nothing to see but the new mask, resting where she thought his lap must be. It was finished; there was not a rough seam remaining to the leather, the agate eyes stared their polished-cedar stare, a smear of powdered carmine and sweat tinted the lips. Dark golden mohair fluffed and tufted around the fox-boned face; it needed only a fine comb to transform it into the soft curls draped before a young woman's ears. Julian found one in a tangle of detail braid and held it out in one cautious hand.

When she bent to offer the comb, Isley popped into view swift as a pantomime devil.

"Love is, itself, the ugliest thing in the world," he announced, flat and bitter. "Having said that, I present you the woman I loved. Not ugly. Not even considering ugliness as a half-time weekend profession. She was one of the more interesting paradoxes of my existence." Isley rose, choreographed-crisp, legs still crossed. He handed Julian the new mask.

It was still pliable, its contours unset, but there was no doubt. She tried to find something to say, or to ask him, but couldn't.

"It's just a girl," she got out finally. "You never make just girls. She's not finished, she's got to be a naiad, or a hama-dryad, or something—"

"Put it on, Julian, please."

The mask touched her, formed her face, and she felt a strange reversal, like a stopping heart, like electric shock. For centuries she had felt herself growing fainter; now the ghost-image that lived only inside her mind was suddenly standing in the middle of the workshop, more solid and real than she had ever been even in life. Her feet were bare, and they were touching the tile floor, and in danger of stepping on a needle. Her elbows strained the sleeves of a smock gone two years too small. Her hair was heavy, not tangled but not washed, either, and she had a moment's idea that she ought to go at it with a duck's egg and some lavender.

"Isley, this can't be right." She turned, slowly, to accustom herself to the weight of a human body. "This is—me."

"Don't worry," he said, deadly soft, "I've had years to get over the blow."

"What? No—Isley, I don't remember—I can't remember us being in love. I'm sorry."

"I don't expect you would." He clutched a handkerchief in his hand and his hand against his throat, as if something truly choked him, and when he spoke his words were tiny cruel punches of air. "You might call it unrequited, I suppose. You died."

Julian sat down on the floor, without remembering to fold at the waist or knees. "What?"

"Gunpowder," Isley said, almost blandly. "I imagine it rather stymied the natives. One can't suppose anyone from Monmouth town ever made it to China, not in those days." He drew his little Q'ing jade snuffbox out of his pocket in a gesture made lofty by long practice. "You thought I got this in an antique barn? A church rummage? A flea market?"

"Isley!" She slid her tongue between her lips to moisten them, biting down as she did. "Start again. Please. With me being dead in England and Chinese gunpowder and you somehow being a part of it, because I don't remember you, I don't. I mean, I don't remember you that way."

His smile was weak. "How could you remember a man who never twice wore the same face? And you must have been, Christ's pity, at most fifteen years old." Isley gave a smooth little shrug, but his shoulders seemed to keep on sinking. "You saw a tailor, a tinsmith, a carver for the church. If you saw me at all."

"But you saw me." The hand closest to reaching for Isley's knotted fast in Julian's skirt. "What happened next?"

"You died," Isley shouted, every false thing stripped from his voice. "You died burning, and all I could do was kill you faster!"

"I think I would have thanked you, if I could."

"You stupid girl, I blew your bloody head off! Am I coming in quite clear?"

"Thank you," Julian said.

Julian sat on a corded-up bale of ancient cotton and around her feet spilled the amber and agates Isley liked to use for eyes. She was winding Isley's last skein of Tyre-dyed silk onto a plain clay bobbin etched with two empty-socket eyes, a worn gashed mouth. When she had wound it once she unspooled it out onto her lap again.

"Julian? My gentian? Is that the door?"

The noise drifted to her, up through the floorboards, so that she imagined him rising like steam. There was no light here, among the bundles of their oldest, choicest, most rare; Isley brought it with him, faintly bluish, as suddenly a piece of fabric stirred from the floor, rose off its bolt, climbed higher to swath an Isley-proportioned mummy.

"You'll have to answer it, darling, I have absolutely nothing to wear in company." The fabric dropped in a heap. "Wrinkled."

"You're ridiculous," she said, though he had gone. She found what she had come for, hours ago, a leather pouch full of opals and a smooth dusky curve of long-seaworn shell. It was old—old, already, when Isley had found it, and across its purples and blue-black nacre someone had scratched a tide's worth of faint waves. She could not have told anyone, or Isley, exactly why she needed it, or what for. The sight of it made her eyes smart and her jaw ache, and in the end it was Isley who answered the door.

She had put on a new mask, one with a sharp strange androgynous face made incongruous by long black curls, and set the bag of opals on her worktable and tucked the polished shell into the pulse-curve of her palm, before she realized that someone besides Isley had made it as far as the kitchen.

"No," Isley was saying, moving like a shell-shocked whirlwind among cups and saucers and the sugar bowl. "No, no, no. You don't get a mask—we don't make a mask for you—it's the rules. The rules! Oh no, no, no, no, no, no, no."

Julian saw his hands, white and quick, now a conjurer's hands, now a supplicant's, and an incredible quantity of Darjeeling sifting from them onto the floor, as she rounded the tight bend of the stairs.

"I'm telling you, you'll have to go. I shan't do business with you, my dear—er—my esteemed—absolutely not."

"Isley—?" Julian's footsteps sounded, to her ears, like giants moving the furniture: Isley and his visitor-intruder had gone silent.

"It was you, then, who left the card?"

"Me?" Julian managed. "Card?" Her mask-lips were moving but the voice could have been a growl or a mew or a peep; from her bitten round fingernail ends to the center of where she thought she recalled her heart, she paid attention to the person speaking.

It had the most beautiful face she had ever seen.

Cities burned there, and lean starveling children looked out, fierce; or it might have been the face of a baby born five minutes before. From one moment to the next the face shifted, pale, crimson, proud, lovely, eyes blue as water or dapple-green as leaves. Julian was going to faint, and regretted not having a body to faint with or blood vessels to effect it. She dropped into the closest chair and waited for time to cross the next moment, and then the stranger was handing her a water-stained, crumpled card. It was her own, bearing three words only.

"Julian Sible," the visitor read aloud, "masks."

Julian nodded. Blink, and the face across from her might be female; but the colors and contours changed so fast, and it was a man again leaning out to her, eyes black as crags.

"How did you find me," she croaked out, "from that?"

"I've been looking for you a very long time. I need a mask, please."

"See here, now, I've told you, you won't find help here. It's not done—not allowed—we can't."

"Yes," Julian agreed. "Yes. Please. I will. Yes."

"Julian!" It was Isley, and the horror in his voice cracked through the small kitchen like lightning. "Julian, there is no mask for—for our guest. Listen. Poppet—" Isley bent and words sizzled beside her ear. "Don't you know who he is? Are you quite mad?"

"She, I think," Julian said, vaguely. "It's all right, Isley." She rubbed his hand, until warmth rose, and then offered her hand to the stranger's cold one. "Your name is all I need to make the mask, but it may never come back to you again."

"I think our visitor understands that, dear heart."

"Yes." Julian's feet could not find the floor, and without Isley to press down on her shoulders she would have slid away into a million loose-flown pieces. The remnant of once-alive hedge-girl deep in her cried 'ware. "But that's exactly what you want, isn't it?"

"I can't get it right."

Isley caught her, when she fell against his bedroom

windowsill; hauling Julian under the arms he pulled her the rest of the way through the window. "I won't ask what you were doing, my truant, on the fortieth foot of that particularly iffy fire escape." Isley scooped, catching the bend of Julian's knees, and carried her to the fire.

He had a fire in every season, though wood and chimney both were lacking. The flames tonight shifted from blue to green to pink, the liquid in the kettle was thick and poppy red, and Julian could not get warm.

"Say again," Isley demanded, filling a cup from the kettle, "whatever compelled you to think the side of our domicile was for climbing, and not for keeping out this blasted snow-crammed wind."

"It won't come right!"

Isley fussed, as well as he could fuss with one arm kept tight around her shoulders. "Ah. The mask, yes. Julian, there are some things in this world, you know, for which, for whom, bleeding hell, there can be no mask."

"I'm cold," Julian choked out. "P-please!"

He took off his lime sateen robe and wrapped her in it. "You kept too long at the work. Was he—was she—was your subject in the room with you, all this time?"

Julian nodded.

"It's a wonder you don't snap into bits like an icicle. Dulcet, even one of the Goddess' deathless bloody own can't bear—"

Julian kissed Isley.

Isley wobbled like a pudding.

"Oh. Child, you can't have meant to do that. You're over-worked. You aren't yourself."

"I'm not myself? Who's that, Isley, tell me!"

"Whoever it is you are when Death isn't sleeping in the downstairs lounge, for pity's sake!" Isley stirred the fire, found his elbows and knees at sudden contrary angles, found Julian's arms were around him and he had to look into Julian's eyes. "Right. Right then, I'll shut up, shall I shut up?"

"I don't think she sleeps." Julian cleared her throat. "But that has nothing to do with anything, and I'm sorry."

"I beg your pardon?"

"I'm sorry for shouting, just now, like that."

"Oh. Ah. Indeed. Yes."

"I came up to talk with you." Julian paused, considered Isley's face. "Are we going to be able to talk, or should I go away?"

"Please don't," Isley managed. "I mean, please stay. Julian."

"Tell me what your life was like," Julian had to brace her knees to keep Isley from turning away. "Before you made the masks."

"Oh, dear. You mean right up to—"

"Yes. Tell me how you died."

"Right. So, there was this river, and it was pretty much the world. And there was this fellow, and he was also pretty much the world, and Julian, glove to my hand, must I go on with this?"

"What was his name?"

"Maatesankh."

"What?"

"Maat, Maatesankh, The-Goddess-of-Truth-Has-Made-Him-Live, if you want to go the long way round."

"Egypt!"

"No, not Egypt, just the river." Isley waved a hand. "It was all I knew or saw of anything that might vaguely have been the world."

"What did you do? I mean, what was the living part like?"

"Doorkeeper of Amun," said Isley, with exactly the inflection of *pass the salt.* "It comes down to being a big hulking sort with a knouted club, only in a temple, with the king's over-spiced corpse on display. To say nothing of the cripples, and the beggars, and the mourners, and the Greeks."

"And Maat?"

"He was a weaver, principal weaver of royal tapestry. He was young. He had beautiful shoulders. He—he passed most of his life in a workshop, down near the shallows. I would beat the tar out of his foreman so he could go home at night. It was all most frightfully romantic. Have you gleaned enough yet? Do you understand enough, now? It was my life. I never looked at it until it was over."

"I'm sorry. It's just, I don't remember what it felt like—" Julian took Isley's hand. "I don't remember what about life made me real."

"Real?" Isley's gaze was so distant Julian thought she could see reeds in it, and a river. "You mean, fleshly real, cut out my heart and hand it to the jackal and look to see if I've felt something? That sort of real?"

"Isley."

His hand over hers was squeezing.

"Isley."

"Why on earth do you want to understand that?"

"Isley!"

Then he jerked her up onto her feet, and with a bang and a patter of dust Isley let down the attic ladder. "Let me show you something. I'm going to show you something, my Julian, and in the end you'll understand. You're going to disappoint Mistress Death no matter what your gift lets you create, because alive and real and human and flesh all end as charcoal and water, and that's not very aesthetically bloody pleasing."

It was thin, whatever he had brought down from the attic. Paper, maybe, papyrus; folded in linen turned amber with age. Julian stood in the weird pinkish firelight, waiting.

It was cloth, not paper, and Julian could make out alabaster white, ochre, green, black, gold from where she stood.

"Closer, then," Isley murmured. "I find it doesn't like the air, or the light."

The bit of weaving was only about the size of a dinner napkin. Two men, hand-high, in Egyptian profile walked the gold sand bordering a blue river; their hands were linked, and tiny hieroglyphs rose out of the same green as the river-reeds.

"I can't read them," Julian whispered, afraid the sound would turn threads into dust. "Please, Isley."

"His name, and my name. Maat-es-ankh, there—and Aiy." One of Isley's long, precise fingers drew across the fabric, never touching it, perhaps.

His fist closed so quickly that Julian took a step back. "Herein lies the lesson: he died for this. He made this, for me, and it was his unmaking."

"Why? Was it—the two of you—forbidden?"

"That, oh, not that. His great crime was stealing all this linen." Isley framed the square within the span of his hands. "This is what a real life is worth. This, here. Although I shouldn't say, exactly, that they killed him."

"What happened to him?"

"They beat him just until blood came and they threw him in the river. Crocodiles. Holy beasts, in the water." For a long moment only Isley's hands spoke, twisting painfully around the air when even his eyes were mute. "Of course I went in after him. I loved him. Nobody stopped me. What else could I do?"

Julian held him, swaying from the waist gently as a reed.

"I saw a face, in the dark, in the water. I prayed with all my worth it would be his." Isley sighed. "It was a mask."

Julian walked fast. No sound but the snow stroking away beneath her shoes, as she crossed the empty street; not even a cab stopped at the light. It was before midday, she knew that, the odd hour between buses emptying and shops filling up; but all the clocks in their house had stopped working.

It was half a mile to the elevated train, and she had no clear idea what to do when she got there. She stood on the sidewalk, choosing her direction, staring up until the light hurt her eyes and a jogger flicked slush that slid down her coat. It was an old black wool coat, with a sole dangling button, and holes showing her shirt at the elbows; Julian took longer than it wanted to brush the gray snow away. Always, now, that crawling, shivering sense of time.

She bought two fares and dropped the change, without looking, beside a girl with willow-green eyes tuning a battered guitar. "Play 'Tempus Est Iocundum', do you know that one?"

"Hey, wait," Julian heard her, but the train was rushing in. "You gave me—hey—you dropped a fifty dollar bill!"

Julian went to Little Saigon, because it was farthest out on the line, and she bought sweet bean cakes for Isley, nearly half a pound. She thought she would stop for a drink or a book but then there was, in the end, no time; only the crush of passengers against her on the train, jarring her mask so she feared showing silvery at the edges, and it was suddenly six o'clock and heavy dusk. Full dark, when she turned her key in the lock and came into the dim entryway. Julian found the closest light switch and all the bulbs showed was the coat rack, Isley's scarlet downstairs slippers, and the shelf of books that had overflowed into the hallway, *Beginning Duets for Kithara and Phorminx* uppermost. Nothing to mark that Death stayed in the house.

"Isley? Hello?"

"Up here, my dulcet, working!"

"Brought you something." Julian peered over Isley's shoulder, draping the white paper bag against his chest.

"Working, my snow-swan, working," he replied. "Set it just there. I'll get to it before long."

She did as she was told, easing aside a few stacked, open books to find a place on the desk. She took more than twice as long as a reasonable person would.

"How's it going, then, the thing for Mistress Death? Not that she eats us out of a house and home, but, floppet, she's rather an unsettling flat-mate. And do you suppose no one's dying, while she's putting her nose in our books? What an awful lot of disorder it must be, out there."

"The same amount as ever," Julian answered. "I wish you would go out. You never go out."

"Don't want to go down to your studio, eh? Well, I'm working, and no one's sorrier than I about it. I can't entertain today."

"You're making work," Julian accused. "You want to see me fail at this, without you."

"I do not. I can't imagine anything more unpleasant than having My Lady Death an unsatisfied customer." Isley turned, taking both her hands in his. "I have no idea what help to give you. Some things in the world, my love, are not meant to wear masks."

"What do I do?"

He had turned back to dabbing paint on a little clay rough-work mask.

"What would you have me do?" A little desperately Julian reached, but he moved before she could catch his shoulder.

"Oh, and Julian? I do hope you'd the wit to ask for the one thing she's got worth having."

Death was watering the strawberry geraniums. She set down the old tin measuring cup at the sound of Julian hitting the kitchen floor with three stairs to spare, and shook her wet hands over the sink, and sat down at the table.

Julian had landed on her feet, but the sight of Death was making her ears ring and her knees sag slightly, and she had to hold tight to the carved lion's head on the balustrade. "Sit down," she said to Death, who was already sitting.

"I," Julian started. "I. The price. What I asked for. It counts for Isley too. Do you understand that? Or you'll leave, you'll go and I'll do everything I can to make sure you never find us again."

Death tucked her long dark hair back from her face. Written across her skin which was no color at all Julian could see red and black and peacock-blue lines, scribbled lines and block-printed lines, X's and handprints. She understood, because Death wanted her to understand. Maybe her own contract was under all of it, somewhere, and Death remembered the terms, and everything was clear as a diamond in ice.

"Say something," Julian begged. "Say yes, no, something, anything!"

Death reached across the table, and shook Julian's hand.

Her hand was not, Julian thought, so cold as most people thought. Julian could feel the faint lines along the palm, and beneath the pressure of her own thumb, a vein. But in Death's veins ran darkness, sorrow and time.

"Julian? It's gone three o'clock."

She turned, pulling her feet back over the keel of the roof. Snow slipped from her shoulders. "I came up to see the stars," Julian explained. "Were they the same, when you were alive?"

"Not entirely." Stiffly Isley lowered himself beside Julian, wincing a little at the shingles against his back. "They did seem brighter then. Closer. But Hathor's still up there, poor old cow, and the Leg of the Sky, and the Chariot."

"They haven't changed, to me," Julian murmured. "I thought I knew so much about them, while I lived, and yet—"

"And yet?"

"Nothing I had learned from them saved me." She looked down at her shoes, soaked through and with ice on the laces. "They burned no witch, Isley, they burned a midwife's 'prentice with a stolen copy of *Gramarye and Astrologie.*"

"Oh, yes, that's all there is to you, I'm sure."

"A hedge-witch then," Julian shrugged.

"Dulcet," said Isley, tartly.

"And I'm sure I don't remember them burning me, besides. I—it seemed to me I woke up in the mask room, with all those faces around me, empty, waiting; and no windows, no stars." She found her balance against Isley's ribs. "Was it the same for you?"

"Nothing was waiting for me." Isley tipped his head back, found a constellation and gave it five minutes of his silence. "The place you call the mask room, yes, but just me, and the one mask. And some instructions, I rather think, somewhere in my head. They're setting," he added, "the stars. Shall we go down, my Julian? Or stay to be modern ice sculpture in the morning?"

"There's just one thing I want to show you," Julian faltered, "I mean, I knew how to do it a very long time ago. I wanted to see if I still could. So I. Well. Give me a second, all right?"

She took off her mask, and dragged enough memory-tatters together to be eyes, and speech, and two upraised hands in the stark moonlight. A spark caught along one palm, rounded out and gained a pinkish-golden tint. It was only the size of a good steady candle flame, but it was intensely bright.

"I wanted to show you a star you knew," Julian explained. "I mean, then."

"Sothis." Isley reached out. "The lady Sothis. I knew her very well. The flood-star, you know."

"I know." Julian closed her hand, and the light went out.

"Beautiful." And Isley cleared his throat. "I should very much like to kiss you," he said, "but—man or woman, I don't know what you—I have no idea what would be right."

"Take off your mask," Julian suggested. "I'll find you."

"The stars again, is it?"

"I keep wondering." Julian spread her fingers, Sirius glinting between them like a gem. "Will they still move the same way, when it's done?"

Isley straddled the peak of the roof. "They have, as long as I—as I've walked. Look, there, the Immovables." And, "what it?"

"The mask."

"Ah. That. Yes."

"What if it changes something? What if the mask is wrong?"

"You've never made a wrong mask."

"What if it's wrong, the whole thing?"

"I had thought of that."

Julian faced Isley. "Tell me."

"I don't know what's going to happen, my emerald. I had imagined—oh—I don't know, an enormous great vacuum or something opening from the sky."

"Nice," Julian said through tight teeth. "And we're just swallowed up, then, the mask room and everything?"

"No. No, I imagine the mask room will still be somewhere, even when you and I are spiraling the cosmos in infinitesimal tiny pieces."

"Do you really think that's what comes after?" Julian reached for Isley's hand, bashed her knuckles on the shingled slant and tucked herself small on the roof-peak instead.

"Child, I don't know." A silence came where breathing might have been. "But think of such things and you'll be no good for the work, it'll be us and Death at dice in the parlor until the world's end."

"It's done." Julian slid her feet onto the uppermost rung of the fire escape.

"I beg your pardon?"

"I finished the mask this afternoon."

Gently Isley laid a hand on the bone latch of the mask room door, and for a moment the darkness hummed, while he stood and half-bowed Julian past him.

Light came, without their knowing. In the center of the room there was calm like the trough of a wave, and scattered around as always, as ever the bales of fabric and wicker hampers of thread. Mask-forms hung the walls, some half clothed, others blank and white as skulls or granite-rough. They all stared, now; and stirred, Julian imagined, with trapped centuries' worth of unbreathed breath.

"Is it the last, I wonder?" Isley followed her gaze, the room's span and back, meeting the naked unfinished faces. "Julian, do you think so?"

"I don't know," Julian heard, and maybe repeated it. "A mask for every person who needs—"

"Yes," Isley cleared his throat on the affirmation, "but, er, this one does seem to cover a lot of ground at once. There was nothing ever said, for the making of this one." His hand came up lightly to her hair. "I would have helped you. You know—"

"I know." Julian, watery, crossed the three steps to her worktable. The mask was there, on its plinth, under cover of plain linen to keep dust and oil from it. Death's mask. Only the master's approval was lacking. "Isley—"

"Will it be your best, then? The pinnacle, the happy ever after?"

Her hand stopped, clenched hard into the fabric, and if sweat had been hers, Julian thought, there would have been a print clear as Veronica. "There are no more, Isley, not in me."

"Oh." Though Isley stood straight and still, Julian saw him crumble, shore in a tide. "Will you—will you excuse me, then, Julian?"

"You're going?" She stared. "Without—you haven't even, I mean, you won't see it, then?"

"Julian, Julian, I will see it, I will scrutinize it, I will do so microscopically and with the greatest relish. Julian," he soothed and patted and fussed with her collar, "Julian."

"I have to know if it's right." Miserable and suffocating in herself she put his hands aside. "I need you to see this one, Isley, without putting it off any longer, or I'm going to go mad and slash it in pieces and there won't be another!"

"I don't think it need come to that. I only wanted a moment to compose myself, you know, but then, I suppose one composes minuets, or salads—"

"Isley!"

At the table's edge he bowed to her again, more distant, more strange than before; so austere he looked, with his gaze dark and sober and his features cold in the lightless light of the mask room, that Julian moved aside for him. Isley's hands drew back the drape.

"Oh."

The face was plain white plaster, painful. Eyes each a single opal threw no single color. When Isley touched the lips, the mouth opened; but no color spread, and the features Julian had molded did not soften. Where hair or headdress might have been was only a starkly folded veil.

"Julian, love, it's rather—"

Julian leaned past him, and with three fingertips brushed the edge of the veil. Isley saw starlight, or a glint on water; color rose, thinly at first, then quickening over the cloth as a flame might spread.

Meadows were there, gold and green and purple; a pale stand of twisted birches, the blue of a river and a slender boat rowing, the breath of its oarsmen steam in a cold morning. Girls danced in gowns of saffron, scarlet, onion-dye yellow, so close and clear that Isley saw the silver pomanders sway at their waists. There were horses, ploughing and pulling and riding to war brightly saddled; farms that faded to thatched towns before rising as glass-faced cities. Isley recognized the train smoking through Siberia and the tilted smoky walls of Buda and Pest; there were swords arrayed near a temple door in Japan, and Julian's favorite flower stall in New York. A feast in five courses, deceptions and ices too; half a torn farl of oaten bread, and something in a carved horn cup; a cauldron hung at the fire-back and the fast sliding pages of queerly figured books. The pictures pooled and muddled but were not still; Isley watched as long as he could, until everything settled blue-black as winter night and sparkling.

"Do you see? Julian?"

Julian's face was pressed into Isley's shirt.

He stepped back, and though her weight followed his for a moment, Julian straightened and pushed the tangle of hair from her face.

"It was all right?"

Isley caught her again and squeezed until Julian's feet left the ground, and she felt sure seams were cracking and mask-spells splintering on both sides. "My darling, darling Julian, I almost wish it wasn't. Weren't. Oh, bloody fucking hell." He turned, one hand covering his face, and in two strides was through the mask room door.

"Isley?"

He was half down the corridor to his own rooms, and Julian knew from the squared set of his back and shoulders that running behind him was no good.

"Isley!"

"Mind you don't leave that door open. Masks flying out into the world ungifted, where would we be then?"

"You're not coming downstairs?"

"I am."

"But—"

"One does like to meet Death properly dressed."

Julian waited in Isley's paisley-draped armchair, a book open unseen on her lap. She had washed her hands, not to mar the white of the mask when it was presented, and that had taken all of five minutes. Isley, dressing, might keep busy until daylight.

The bedroom door opened and Isley was there.

"I—I thought there would be a sword. Or something—" Julian rose. Only plain sandals on his feet, instead, and a kilt of linen so transparent and fine that even with its thousands of pleatings she could make out the honey color of skin beneath it. A red faience ankh crowned with an eye rested on Isley's chest, and that was all.

The body was taller and better muscled than anything she'd ever seen Isley choose, and the head was starkly shaved, though she had never seen a mask of his without elaborate or fanciful hair. There was no orange, no magenta, just that pleasant reddish-honey tone of the skin, and the eyes were dark, maybe brown tourmaline—

Julian blinked. Stared, searching for the edges, and did not find them. This was a better mask-making than any she knew. Then Isley moved, towards her, and when Julian saw him move she had to sit down again.

"No mask," she got out, around the sand and thorns, "you're not wearing a mask."

"Boo," Isley shrugged, mildly.

"I thought you had forgotten yourself—I mean, I've never seen—"

"Despite my best efforts, darling Julian, myself has not managed to be forgotten." He offered his arm, and she levered herself from the chair with it; Isley's memory-body was solid, as her own had never been. Julian did not clear his shoulder.

"Not so bad, is it?"

"N-nice. Yourself— is nice."

"Miss Wyckes," Isley cleared his throat. "Shall we?"

She did not remember entering the mask room, that last time, as she could not remember the first; somehow she was down the stairs to the kitchen, with Isley, or Aiy, behind her. The mask was balanced between her hands, so she must have gone to the mask room, but Isley had opened and shut the door. And now there were no more doors, no more blind steps guided by Isley's hand at her back; Julian stood near the sink and the sun was rising and she did not have to move again. Death's eyes were on her, which was what made the idea of stirring another step so very hard, and Isley's eyes were on Death. Julian could read them, clear as if the words there were only kept behind glass: harm her and I will kill you. For the half-split of a second she wondered on the killing of Death.

Isley's hand had not left her. Julian managed a step forward, and put the mask in Death's hand.

"Your name I take as payment," said Julian. "Name your-self now, as you will."

Death put on the mask, and there was no time to get out of the way.

She saw the white flare and felt the faint heat that came with mask-spells sealing; then the kitchen filled with a rank metal smell of wrong. Isley spoke, words of protection, of binding and quenching, but in the end all she heard was *Julian!* And when they fell, they landed together.

All the windows had flown open, the cabinet hinges had fallen apart and the locks on the back door were melted into runny pudding. Confused spells had scorched the wallpaper and there was a scrap of Death's black cashmere sweater still floating in lazy spirals to the floor. Death and the mask were gone.

"Isley?" Julian had to spit out something that tasted of copper and salt. "Are you here? D'it work?"

"Hold still." Isley rolled away from her and sat upright. "Hold still. You're bleeding. You know, with blood."

"You, too." Julian reached to blot Isley's shoulder, where their weight had met the wall and splintered wood.

"I'll survive, I think. I do confess I'm not very sure about the kitchen."

"I'm sorry about your Dresden," Julian sniffled, knocking blood from her nose with one wrist and holding herself up with the other.

"Oh, I don't think your spells did that," Isley said, nudging aside a few fragments of the Dutch oven. "I mean, give a mask to one of the Goddess' deathless own, and one's bound to lose something. In the old days it would have been, I don't know, something soft and wet. For instance a heart." He paused, hauling her out of the table's shadow to peer at her face. "Julian, are you okay, love?"

"I just, I need to stand up. I need to know it worked. If—what I asked for—if it worked."

"It worked, as ever, because it must and it has to, darling Julian." On his feet now, it was a minute before Isley pulled Julian after him; he still gazed uneasily at the ceiling's cross-beams as he spoke. "Rules, you know."

"But," Julian started. Isley beckoned her, before she could finish properly, to the kitchen window.

The sun had climbed, and in the soft earth of their ragged herb-garden Julian saw footprints. They stopped at the alley fence, but caught there between earth and sky on a sharp chain link was a scrap of something dark blue, that shimmered like the sea at nightfall and then, suddenly, was no longer there at all.

"And so Death got away," Isley intoned, "and they all lived happily ever after. Or the shoddy bloody kitchen caved in and killed them, whichever you like."

"Isley, what happens now?"

"Poor girl, she'll probably tread out her life as a stock-broker, or an astrophysicist, or something hopelessly mundane like that. And be happy as anyone living has right to be, with perhaps a little peace thrown in, just for sauce. It was a good mask, Julian, darling. She'll make it work out."

"I meant, to us."

"Well, *us* is a nice enough thought to be going on with. Don't you think?"

STORY NOTE

This came about because of a mask. It was the blank white form of a face, with words written all across it in strange alphabets and inks; and that image stayed a long time in my head. I wanted to work with how and why we use masks, and what we change or signify by their use. Gender, orientation, beauty, identity and memory are all tied together in the faces we choose for display.

And what if you had gone on so long that your memory held more than twenty lifetimes' worth of faces, and you could show us any one of them at all, or none?

So I had to write the story.

Printed in the United States
43376LVS00001B/44